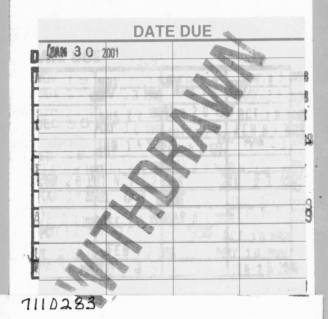

ALICE ANN
Gets Ready for School

CYNTHIA JABAR

Little, Brown and Company
Boston   Toronto   London

First edition

Library of Congress Cataloging-in-Publication Data

Jabar, Cynthia.
   Alice Ann gets ready for school / Cynthia Jabar.
      p.   cm.
   Summary: Alice Ann experiences both fun and
anxiety as she gets ready for the biggest event in her life.
   ISBN 0-316-43457-4   88-37988
   [1. Schools — Fiction.] I. Title.   CIP
PZ7.J128A1   1989   AC

10 9 8 7 6 5 4 3 2 1

WOR

Joy Street Books are published by
Little, Brown and Company (Inc.)

Published simultaneously in Canada
by Little, Brown & Company (Canada) Limited

Printed in the United States of America

*For my mother and father
and with special thanks
to Melanie*

I'm going to school this year!

My friend Juanita already goes to school. She says my teacher, Miss Shay, is the best. We'll get to do a different art project every day!

Only seven more days to go. I still have a lot to do.

On Monday Mom takes me shopping.

I try on red shoes,   silly shoes,

grown-up shoes,   bouncy shoes,

and perfect shoes.

On Tuesday I find the only tyrannosaurus lunchbox.

On Wednesday Juanita comes over to see my new
shoes. We practice school. I'm the teacher this
time, and she's my helper.

On Thursday Dad brings home notebooks for us.
I pick yellow and red — my favorite colors.

On Friday we take a walk to see my school.
"It looks so BIG," I say to Mom. "I know," she tells
me, "but everyone will be friendly and helpful."

On Saturday Grammy and Grampy come over. Grampy tells stories about when he was in school. Once his teacher made him write his name five hundred times until he got it just right.

On Sunday I show Mom how I can write my name.

"Great job," she tells me.

When it's time for my bath, Liza says I can use her Supersuds.

I use just enough to get really clean.

After I get into my pj's I check to see if my
shoes still fit.

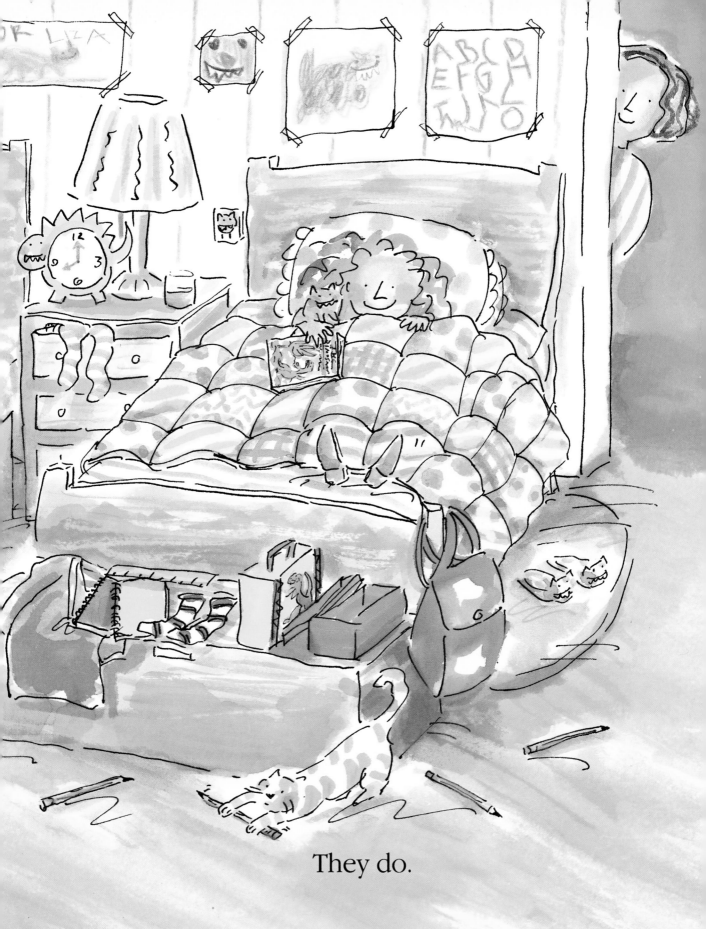

They do.

Dad and Mom read me my favorite story.

Then it's time to go to sleep. Mom tucks me in. Dad says, "Sleep tight, Alice Ann. Tomorrow's your big day!"

I'm still awake when Liza climbs into bed. I keep wondering what school will be like tomorrow.

I can't sleep.
"Liza? Liza, what if I miss the bus?" I ask.
"Don't worry," she tells me, "you won't. We all take the same bus."

Now I'm worried I won't be able to find my classroom.
"Liza, I'll be lost," I say.

"Juanita said she will show you where your classroom is. Tomorrow will be a wonderful day, Alice Ann. Now let's get some sleep," she says.

Liza! Time to get up! Today is my first day
of school.

I'm the first one dressed. When I'm done, my sister Holly braids my hair.

"Mom! Dad! Look! I'm all ready for school," I say.
"Wonderful!" says Mom.
"And so early," Dad says.

Before breakfast my baby brother Jasper helps me pack my knapsack.
"Thanks for helping," I say. "Would you like one of my new pencils?"

At breakfast I'm not very hungry. Mom says, "Drink your juice and eat your toast, it's a long time until lunch." When Dad hands me my lunchbox, I peek inside. The sandwich is peanut butter and banana, my favorite!

"Time for pictures," Mom says.
"Smile, Alice Ann," says Dad.

"Bye, Mom, bye, Dad, bye, Jasper," I say.

Juanita saved me a seat.
I'm on my way to school!